It's Mine!

"That unicorn is mine," Lila shouted. "Give it back."

Amy shook her head. "It's mine," she said.

"I *know* it's mine," Lila said in a know-it-all voice. "I can tell just by looking at it."

"But we couldn't tell them apart before," Elizabeth reminded Lila. "They're identical. Let's just look for the other one."

"Why should I have to look for Lila's unicorn?" Amy said.

"Are you sure it's yours, Amy?" Eva asked timidly.

Instead of answering, Amy hugged the unicorn tight.

Elizabeth looked at Jessica. Their slumber party was ruined!

SWEET VALLEY KIDS

SWEET VALLEY SLUMBER PARTY

Written by
Molly Mia Stewart

Created by
FRANCINE PASCAL

Illustrated by
Ying-Hwa Hu

A BANTAM SKYLARK BOOK®
NEW YORK · TORONTO · LONDON · SYDNEY · AUCKLAND

RL 2, 005–008

SWEET VALLEY SLUMBER PARTY
A Bantam Skylark Book / September 1991

*Produced by Daniel Weiss Associates, Inc.
33 West 17th Street
New York, NY 10011*

Cover art by Susan Tang

ISBN 0-553-15934-8

Published simultaneously in the United States and Canada

PRINTED IN THE UNITED STATES OF AMERICA

CWO   0 9 8 7 6 5 4 3 2 1

To Margaret Abigail Chardiet

CHAPTER 1

Great-Aunt Helen

Elizabeth Wakefield opened her closet and took out her sleeping bag.

"What are you doing?" asked her twin sister, Jessica. "Our slumber party isn't until tomorrow night."

"I know," Elizabeth said. "But I think we should start getting ready." She unrolled the sleeping bag on the floor and got inside. "I'm so excited," she said. "This is our first slumber party, and it's going to be so much fun."

"We've had a sleep-over before," Jessica reminded her. "Remember our camp-out?"

"I know, but this is different." Elizabeth zipped up her sleeping bag and snuggled inside. "This one will be indoors and this time Steven won't be around to bother us."

"I'm glad he's staying with Grandma and Grandpa this weekend," Jessica said.

Jessica and Elizabeth's older brother, Steven, had sprayed the tent with water while the twins and their friends were sleeping inside. He had almost ruined the camp-out.

"I guess I'll get my sleeping bag out now, too," Jessica said.

Jessica and Elizabeth were identical twins and they often did the same things. It was as if they each had a built-in best friend. They were the only twins in the second grade at Sweet Valley Elementary School. They looked exactly alike, with blue-green eyes and long blond hair with bangs. They often wore the

2

same outfits, but Elizabeth liked most of her clothes to be green, while Jessica usually chose pink.

Elizabeth and Jessica were alike in a lot of ways but they were different in a lot of ways, too. Elizabeth liked reading and making up stories, and she enjoyed her classes at school. She was on a soccer team, too, and she loved to play outside, even if it meant getting dirty.

Jessica was the opposite. She hated to get her clothes dirty. In fact, she didn't like playing outdoors at all. She preferred to stay inside and play with her dolls and stuffed animals. She thought the best parts about school were recess and talking with her friends.

"Are you snug as a bug?" Elizabeth asked. Jessica had zipped her sleeping bag up to her chin.

3

"Yes!" Jessica answered. "I don't think I'll ever come out."

The door of their bedroom opened, and Mrs. Wakefield came in. She laughed when she saw them on the floor in their sleeping bags. "Isn't it a little early for that?" she said. "The slumber party isn't until tomorrow."

"We're just practicing," Jessica explained.

Mrs. Wakefield sat on Jessica's bed. "I'm sorry Dad and I won't be here," she said. "I know you'll have a wonderful time with Great-Aunt Helen, though."

Mr. and Mrs. Wakefield were going away for the weekend on a business trip. Mrs. Wakefield's aunt was coming to stay with the twins while their parents were gone.

"Mom?" Elizabeth asked. "Will you call us while you're away?" She felt a little nervous.

Mrs. Wakefield sat down on the floor be-

4

tween the twins. "Of course I will. But you'll be too busy even to think about us. Besides, you'll love Great-Aunt Helen. She's always been my favorite aunt."

Jessica sat down on her bed next to Mrs. Wakefield. "But what if something goes wrong? Great-Aunt Helen won't know what to do," she said.

"Yes, she will," Mrs. Wakefield said. "I promise. She always took very good care of me when I was a little girl."

Elizabeth was curious about Great-Aunt Helen. She was their mother's aunt, and she was also Grandma Robertson's sister. Elizabeth thought Great-Aunt Helen must be a very old woman.

"I hope I like her," Jessica said.

They heard a car stop in the driveway. Then a horn honked. Mrs. Wakefield gave

5

each twin a hug. "That must be her. Come on, let's put on happy faces and go meet her."

Elizabeth and Jessica looked at each other. It would seem funny to be at home without their parents. They both crossed their fingers for luck and followed their mother downstairs.

"Hello, Alice!" they heard a cheerful voice say.

Elizabeth peeked into the hallway. Their mother was hugging a plump woman with white hair and glasses. The woman looked at Elizabeth and winked.

"Hello," she said.

Elizabeth pulled Jessica with her into the hall. "Hi," they both said to Great-Aunt Helen.

"Hmm, let me see," Great-Aunt Helen said, putting one finger on her chin. "You're

6

Elizabeth, and you're Jessica." She pointed to each twin.

"That's right!" Elizabeth said.

"How could you tell?" Jessica asked.

"I'm a good guesser," Great-Aunt Helen said. "I haven't seen you girls since you were babies."

Jessica looked at her seriously. "We're not babies anymore. We're in second grade."

"Of course you aren't babies," Great-Aunt Helen said. "I can see that you two are pretty grown-up."

Elizabeth smiled. She liked Great-Aunt Helen already.

CHAPTER 2

Twin Unicorns

Jessica stood at the living room window on Saturday afternoon. Mr. and Mrs. Wakefield had just left on their trip. Jessica was watching the street, so she could see her friends the moment they arrived.

A car stopped in the driveway. "Lila and Ellen are here!" Jessica called out, running to the door.

Another car pulled up behind the first one, and Amy Sutton and Eva Simpson got out. Lila Fowler, Ellen Riteman, Amy, and Eva waved good-bye to their parents, and then they all walked up to the house together.

"You guys brought a lot of stuff," Elizabeth said when she saw them. "Put everything in the den. That's where we'll be sleeping."

The girls put their sleeping bags and suitcases and pillows in the den. Great-Aunt Helen came downstairs to say hello.

"This is Lila and Ellen and Eva and Amy," Jessica said.

"I'm very glad to meet you all," Great-Aunt Helen said with a big smile. "You all get settled. I'll be upstairs if you need me."

Lila was already piling her things up neatly. "This is a brand-new sleeping bag," she said proudly.

"Wow! It's purple," Ellen said. "Can I try it out?"

"Not right now." Lila put her pillow on top of her sleeping bag. "I don't want it to get ruined."

"What should we do first?" Jessica asked.

"Let's arrange our sleeping bags the way we want to sleep," Eva suggested.

"I'm not sleeping by the window!" Ellen said quickly. "A burglar might come in and step on me."

Everyone laughed. "If a burglar stepped on me, I would bite him in the leg," Amy boasted.

"I'm sleeping next to Elizabeth," Jessica said. She smiled at her sister.

Elizabeth smiled back. "This is going to be so much fun," she said.

Their friends opened their suitcases. Eva took out her favorite stuffed horse. "I brought Arabella," she said.

"That reminds me!" Lila spoke up quickly. "Look at what I got today." She opened a zipper compartment in her suitcase and took

11

out a small, stuffed unicorn. "Isn't that nice?"

"I have one just like it!" Amy said. She opened her blue duffel bag and pulled out an identical toy unicorn.

"Look," Jessica said. "They're identical twins, just like me and Elizabeth."

"You can't tell them apart," Ellen agreed.

Lila frowned. "Mine is better," she said. "It's brand-new, and I got it at the best toy store in the mall."

"I got mine at the mall, too," Amy said. "And mine is *almost* brand-new. It isn't dirty or anything."

Elizabeth looked from one unicorn to the other. "You can't tell them apart," she said.

"I call mine Princess," Amy said proudly. She made Princess trot across her lap.

Jessica looked at the unicorns, too. She

thought they were very pretty. They had silky manes and tails and white horns.

"What's wrong?" Ellen asked Lila. "You look grouchy."

"I am not grouchy," Lila said folding her arms and pouting.

Amy smiled. "She's just upset because we both have the same unicorn."

"Why?" Jessica asked. "Liz and I have lots of the same toys, and we don't care."

Lila stood up and walked out of the room. The others were silent.

Jessica followed Lila into the living room. The slumber party would be ruined if she was grumpy all night.

Lila was sitting on the couch. "Are you mad?" Jessica asked.

Lila lifted her chin up in the air. "Amy is spoiling everything," she said.

Jessica shrugged her shoulders. Lila was her best friend after Elizabeth, but she could be a show-off sometimes. She always liked to be the best at everything. "Let's just have fun, OK?" Jessica said.

Lila looked angry for a moment. "Well, OK," she said finally. "I don't care if Amy has a unicorn, too. *I* know mine is better."

"Good!" Jessica smiled in relief. The slumber party wasn't ruined after all.

CHAPTER 3

Pillow Fight!

Elizabeth tossed her toy koala bear into the air and caught it. "My bear can fly," she said.

"Watch this," Eva said. She sent Arabella flying across the den. Arabella bounced off the couch onto the floor, and the girls started giggling.

Jessica and Lila walked back into the den. "Look," Amy said, laughing. "Our animals can fly!" She threw her unicorn over her head and caught it.

"Our pillows can fly, too!" Ellen shouted.

She picked up her pillow and tossed it at Jessica.

Suddenly, nightgowns, stuffed animals, socks, and pillows were flying back and forth across the room. Everyone was laughing and shouting at the same time. Elizabeth screamed as Jessica hit her on the head with a pillow.

"Pillow fight!" Jessica yelled. She ran out of the room. The rest of the girls chased after her. They raced through the rooms, trying to hit each other with their toys and pillows.

Elizabeth turned the corner and started to run up the stairs. She almost bumped into Great-Aunt Helen, who was standing on the steps.

"My goodness! What's all the noise?" Great-Aunt Helen asked.

"I'm sorry. We were just playing." Elizabeth said, trying to catch her breath. "Let's go upstairs, everyone."

Great-Aunt Helen smiled and headed toward the kitchen. The girls trooped up the stairs together. Lila stopped in front of Mr. and Mrs. Wakefield's room. "Hey, look at those dresses!" she said in an excited voice.

Jessica followed her in. "Those are our mother's best party dresses," she said.

"Why are they out on the bed?" Amy said.

They all crowded around the bed to look at the dresses more closely. One was made of black velvet, another had blue sequins on top, and a third had lace on the collar and cuffs.

"They're so beautiful. Can we try them on?" Lila asked. She didn't wait for an answer as she unzipped the blue sequined dress and stepped into it.

Elizabeth frowned. "I don't think we should touch Mom's clothes," she began.

"Mom lets us sometimes," Jessica said, looking at her sister.

"Maybe if we're careful," Elizabeth said slowly.

"Good. I love playing dress-up," Ellen said eagerly. She grabbed the velvet dress and pulled it on over her jeans.

"Look at me!" Lila said, twirling around. "I feel like a princess."

Elizabeth smiled. She loved trying on her mother's fancy clothes, too. But there were only three dresses out, so Elizabeth and the others just watched as Lila, Ellen, and Eva tried them on.

"Can we put on makeup, too?" Lila asked. The long sleeves of the dress hung down past her fingers.

"Sure," Jessica said. "Come on."

The girls ran into the bathroom. "We can only use lipstick," Elizabeth said. "That's all Mom ever lets us use."

"I like this color," Ellen said, opening a red lipstick. She began to put it on.

"I want that color," Lila said. As she stepped closer to Ellen, she tripped on the hem of the dress. There was a loud noise that sounded like *RIIIIIP!*

Everyone froze. Elizabeth gulped and stared at Lila. "What happened?" she whispered.

Lila's face turned bright pink. "I tore the dress. I didn't mean to," she said.

Jessica kneeled down and looked at the hem of Lila's dress. Part of the hem was torn.

"This is Mom's favorite dress," Jessica said

in a frightened voice. "We're going to get in trouble!"

"Oh, no," Eva said nervously.

"Can we fix it?" Lila asked. She sounded like she was going to cry.

Elizabeth felt terrible. She knew that things had gotten out of control. Her mother would be angry at them.

Suddenly the telephone rang.

"Elizabeth! Jessica!" Great-Aunt Helen called from downstairs. "Your mother is on the phone!"

Elizabeth stared at Jessica. "What should we do?" she asked.

CHAPTER 4

Dress-Up Disaster

Jessica felt her stomach do a swan dive. "We have to talk to her," she whispered. "Come on."

The girls tiptoed back into the bedroom. There was a phone on one of the night tables. Jessica picked up the receiver and held it a little bit away from her ear so that Elizabeth could listen, too.

"Hi, Mom," the two girls said at the same time.

"Hi, girls," Mrs. Wakefield said. "Are your friends all there?"

"Yes," Jessica said. She looked at the bathroom. The others were looking at the torn hem of Mrs. Wakefield's dress. Jessica felt her face turning red. She didn't want to tell her mother about the dress.

"Are you having a good time?" their mother asked.

"Sure, Mom," Jessica said. "We're having a lot of fun."

"Is anything wrong?" Mrs. Wakefield asked. "You sound a little funny."

"Nothing's wrong, Mom," Jessica said quickly. She looked at Elizabeth. "We just had a pillow fight."

"That must have been a sight to see," Mrs. Wakefield said, laughing. "Just make sure you don't get too wild. I don't want to find the house full of broken lamps and vases when I get home."

Elizabeth didn't laugh. "We didn't *break* anything. But Mom—"

"I miss you, Mom!" Jessica said quickly. She wanted to interrupt her sister before she told their mother anything.

"I miss you, too, girls," Mrs. Wakefield said. "Now have a good time. And we'll see you when we get home tomorrow. Bye-bye."

"Bye, Mom." Jessica hung up the phone.

"We should have told her," Elizabeth said.

Jessica looked nervous. "I know, but maybe we can fix it ourselves."

"Did you tell her about the dress?" Lila asked as she came out of the bathroom.

"No," Elizabeth said.

Jessica kneeled in front of Lila again and looked at the ripped hem. "I know where Mom keeps her needles and thread," she said.

"My mother showed me how to sew," Eva told them. "I could try to sew it up."

The girls were all gathered around Lila. Suddenly, Jessica heard a noise out in the hall. She turned around quickly.

Great-Aunt Helen was standing in the doorway. "Dressing up?" she asked. "I used to do that when I was a little girl."

"Um . . . yes," Jessica said. She tried to stand in front of Lila. Eva was trying to take off her dress without being noticed. Amy was staring at the floor. Lila sniffled.

"I thought it sounded a little too quiet up here," Great-Aunt Helen said. She smiled. "First you were screaming downstairs. And then you were quiet as mice. I figured I'd better see what kind of mischief you girls are up to."

Suddenly, Lila burst into tears. The others

looked at each other. They knew they were about to get in trouble.

"What's wrong?" Great-Aunt Helen said, sounding surprised. "I was just teasing."

"This dress got ripped," Elizabeth explained, pointing at Lila.

"I didn't mean to rip it!" Lila sobbed.

Jessica felt terrible for her friend.

"Let me see," Great-Aunt Helen said. She sat on the bed and pulled Lila close. Then she turned up the hem and looked at it closely. "Now, stop crying, dear. Everything is going to be all right."

"But it's ripped," Elizabeth said. "There's no way we can fix it."

Great-Aunt Helen winked at her. "Maybe you can't, but I can. Your mother asked me if I could shorten all of these dresses while I'm here. I'm very good at sewing."

"Is that why they were out on the bed?" Jessica asked.

"That's right." Great-Aunt Helen looked at the torn dress again. "And you've started my work for me. I was going to cut the bottom off anyway, so I could hem it up shorter."

"Really?" Lila gasped.

Great-Aunt Helen gave them all a big smile. "Really. You had a narrow escape this time, but maybe you shouldn't play with such delicate things from now on."

Jessica breathed a huge sigh of relief. "We never ever, ever will," she said.

CHAPTER 5

The Missing Unicorn

"That was a close call," Elizabeth said, leading the way downstairs.

Amy looked around the living room. "We made a real mess."

"Maybe we should put all this stuff back in the den," Eva suggested.

The girls started picking up the pillows, nightgowns, and stuffed animals that were scattered around the room. They carried everything back into the den.

"Let's just stay in the den now," Elizabeth said. "Because we—"

"That's mine, Amy," Lila broke in sharply.

Everyone turned and looked at Amy. She was holding one of the stuffed unicorns. "No, this one is mine," she said.

"No it isn't," Lila said. She held out her hand. "Give it back."

Elizabeth looked at Amy and then at Lila. "Yours is here somewhere, Lila," she said.

"But Lila says that one *is* hers," Jessica said.

Eva shook her head. "Amy says it's *hers*."

"I know it's mine," Lila said in a know-it-all voice. "I can tell just by looking at it."

"But we couldn't tell them apart before," Elizabeth reminded Lila. "They're identical. Let's just look for the other one, OK?"

Elizabeth got down on her knees and started looking under sleeping bags. "Come on, everyone," Elizabeth pleaded. She hated to see her friends arguing. "Help me look for it."

"Why should I have to look for Lila's unicorn?" Amy said.

"You're holding *my* unicorn," Lila insisted. "So you'll be looking for yours."

Ellen and Eva looked confused. They didn't know who to believe.

Elizabeth looked inside the sleeping bags and under the pillows on the floor. The missing unicorn had to be nearby. It couldn't have just disappeared.

"Come on," Jessica said. "Let's look."

Lila made a face and lifted up a cushion on the couch. "I know that unicorn is mine," she said.

Amy made a face, too. "Is not."

"Are you sure, Amy?" Eva asked timidly. "They do look exactly alike."

31

Instead of answering, Amy just hugged the unicorn tight.

Elizabeth felt worse and worse. She knew there was always some way to tell people apart. She and Jessica looked exactly alike, but they usually wore their name bracelets. And their personalities were very different. But toys didn't have personalities. Elizabeth knew there was no way at all to tell the two unicorns apart.

One by one, the girls stopped searching. Amy sat down on her sleeping bag, still hugging the unicorn. Eva sat beside her.

Lila and Ellen sat on the couch with their arms crossed and stared at Amy. Jessica and Elizabeth stood in the middle of the room. Elizabeth looked at her sister. Their slumber party was ruined.

"Let's ask Great-Aunt Helen for help," Elizabeth said.

"Good idea," Jessica agreed. "I'll go get her." She ran out of the room.

"Jessica tells me you have a problem," Great-Aunt Helen said as Jessica dragged her into the room a moment later. "What is it?"

Elizabeth began. "Amy and Lila each brought a stuffed unicorn, but now we can only find one. And now they both want that one."

"We probably threw it somewhere during our pillow fight," Jessica explained. "But now Amy's unicorn is missing."

"You mean Lila's unicorn," Amy said.

"Now, now," Great-Aunt Helen said. "The thing to do is to search the house. After all,

you were running around so much that it could be anywhere. You'll just have to discuss it together and make a plan. In the meantime, I'll hold on to this," she said, taking the unicorn out of Amy's hands.

"But—" Amy blurted out.

"But—" Lila cried.

"I'll just hang on to this so there isn't any more bickering," Great-Aunt Helen said firmly.

"That sounds fair," Elizabeth said. She smiled at the others hopefully.

All she saw were grouchy looks.

CHAPTER 6

A Grumpy Pizza Dinner

"Some of us should look in here again, and some of us should look in the living room," Jessica said.

Nobody moved for a moment. Finally, Elizabeth walked out of the den. The rest of the girls looked at each other. Then, Amy and Eva quickly followed Elizabeth.

"I know it's mine," Lila announced.

"I believe you," Ellen said.

Jessica looked in the wastebasket. It was full of crumpled papers and no unicorn. "You all have to help, you know," she said, opening a drawer in the desk.

"How could it get in there?" Lila asked.

Jessica shrugged. "I don't know."

Lila sat on the couch with a grumpy expression on her face while Jessica and Ellen searched the den. Jessica was starting to feel grumpy, too. Lila wouldn't even help look, and it was her unicorn that had caused the problem! Jessica sat down on her sleeping bag and folded her arms.

"I can't find it anywhere," she said. "But at least I tried."

"Maybe the others found it," Ellen said hopefully.

Lila didn't say anything.

Jessica, Ellen, and Lila walked into the living room. They could see that the others hadn't found the unicorn, either. Everyone looked gloomy.

"Now what are we going to do?" Jessica asked.

Great-Aunt Helen came in from the kitchen. "Any luck?" she asked.

All the girls shook their heads.

"Well this should cheer everyone up," Great-Aunt Helen said. "I ordered two pizzas for dinner, and they'll be here very soon."

"Pizzas?" Elizabeth repeated. Her eyes brightened. But then she looked sad again. Normally, they would all cheer at the idea of having pizzas for dinner. But now they were too crabby to be excited.

While Elizabeth, Amy, Eva, and Ellen went into the kitchen, Jessica stayed behind. She took Lila's hand and led her back to the den.

"I want to ask you something," she said.

"What?" Lila asked.

Jessica glanced at the door and lowered her voice. "Did you hide Amy's unicorn? I know you don't want her to have the same toy as you."

"No!" Lila said, shaking her head from side to side. "She lost it. Besides, I wouldn't do something like that."

Jessica wasn't so sure. "Promise?" she asked.

"Promise." Lila crossed her heart.

Jessica smiled. "OK. I believe you. Amy loses her things all the time, anyway."

"That's right," Lila agreed. "She's always asking to borrow pencils in class."

Jessica believed her friend was telling the truth. But that didn't solve the problem. They were still missing one unicorn. She didn't know what they were going to do.

"Let's go," she said. "I heard the door bell ring, so the pizzas must be here."

The girls went into the kitchen. Two steaming mushroom and pepperoni pizzas were on the table. Everyone started eating, but nobody was talking. From time to time, one of the girls looked at the refrigerator. The unicorn that Great-Aunt Helen had taken from Amy was sitting on top. Jessica picked up a second piece of pizza and put it on her plate. "Where's Great-Aunt Helen?" she asked.

"I don't know," Elizabeth said. "I think she's in the living room."

"Maybe she can help us look for the unicorn," Jessica said.

Great-Aunt Helen was going to hem the ripped dress, and she had ordered pizzas for dinner without even being asked. Jessica de-

cided that her mother had been right about Great-Aunt Helen. Jessica was sure that Great-Aunt Helen could solve any problem.

And if she didn't solve the unicorn problem soon, the twins' slumber party was going to be a disaster.

"I see a lot of long faces in here," Great-Aunt Helen said, coming into the kitchen. "I think I know how to change that." She took a deep breath and smiled. "I know where the missing unicorn is!"

CHAPTER 7

The Unicorn Hunt

"Where?" everyone asked at once.

"Tell us!" Jessica begged.

"Not so fast," Great-Aunt Helen said. She pulled out a chair and sat down. "I can't just tell you like that."

Elizabeth blinked. Great-Aunt Helen was full of surprises. Now Elizabeth could see why Great-Aunt Helen was her mother's favorite aunt.

"I think the thing to do is have a race," Great-Aunt Helen said in a thoughtful voice. She nodded. "Yes, that's right. A scavenger-hunt race. We'll have two teams, and I'll give you a clue."

"We'll be a team," Jessica said quickly, pointing to herself, Lila, and Ellen.

Great-Aunt Helen shook her head. "I'll pick the teams. Elizabeth will be with Lila and Eva. And Jessica, you'll be with Amy and Ellen."

Elizabeth glanced at Lila. She wasn't sure she wanted bossy Lila on her team. Everyone looked uncertain. Amy frowned at Jessica, and Ellen crossed her arms stubbornly.

"The team that solves the riddle and finds the unicorn gets to pick where we go for dessert," Great-Aunt Helen added.

"The ice cream parlor!" Amy shouted.

"Cookie Castle!" Ellen squealed.

"The team that wins gets to decide," Great-Aunt Helen repeated.

44

Elizabeth couldn't wait to get started. "What's the riddle?" she asked.

Great-Aunt Helen leaned closer and raised one finger in the air. "What leans over but doesn't fall? Look near this for the missing doll," she said mysteriously. "That's your only clue."

The girls all stared at her. "That's the clue?" Jessica said.

Elizabeth's imagination began to race. What could lean over without falling? She loved riddles, but this sounded like a tough one!

"Come on," she said to her team. Lila and Eva followed her into the living room.

"What do you think it could be?" Lila asked. She picked up a book from the coffee table and stood it on its end. "This can lean," she pointed out, pushing it with her finger.

"But it falls," Eva said as the book toppled over.

"It must be something that can balance," Elizabeth said. She sat down on the recliner and scratched her head. "What can balance?"

"A seesaw," Eva said.

"But you can't find a seesaw in a house," Lila pointed out. She looked like she was about to start crying.

Elizabeth shook her head. "No. But we have a rocking chair in my bedroom. It leans over, but it doesn't fall."

"That's it!" Lila said, cheering up. "Let's go look!"

They raced upstairs. They could hear Jessica, Ellen, and Amy running from room to room below.

"Hurry!" Eva giggled. "They might find it before we do!"

Elizabeth raced into her bedroom. The rocking chair was by the window. They looked on the seat and on the floor all around the chair, but they didn't see the missing unicorn anywhere.

"We didn't even come in here when we had the pillow fight," Lila said.

Elizabeth laughed. "You're right. I was so sure it was the rocking chair that I forgot."

"What else could the clue mean?" Eva wondered out loud.

"Let me think," Elizabeth said, squeezing her eyes shut. She was trying to picture things in her house that leaned over and balanced. "I know! Hurry!"

"What is it?" Lila asked as they ran into the hall.

"It's—" Elizabeth began.

Then she quickly snapped her mouth shut.

Jessica, Amy, and Ellen were running up the stairs.

"Did you find it?" Amy asked, catching her breath.

"Not yet," Eva said.

The two teams stared at each other. Everyone had pink cheeks from running around the house, and they were all smiling from the excitement of the hunt. Even Lila looked like she was having fun.

"We're going to find it first," Jessica said.

Lila giggled. "No way! Elizabeth, Eva, and I are going to win."

They all watched each other carefully for a moment. Then the two teams ran in opposite directions. Each of the girls wanted to be on the team that solved the riddle and found the unicorn.

CHAPTER 8

A New Clue

Jessica, Ellen, and Amy ran into Mr. and Mrs. Wakefield's bedroom. The party dresses were piled neatly on the bed again.

"Did we bring any stuff when we came in here?" Jessica asked her teammates.

"I don't think so," Ellen said. "But I can't remember."

"I don't see anything in here that leans over but doesn't fall," Amy said.

They all stood in the middle of the room, thinking hard. Jessica stared at the table on her mother's side of the bed.

"Look!" she said, pointing to a lamp that was clamped onto the table. It could lean way over in different positions without falling, because it was attached to the edge of the table.

"Maybe the unicorn is here!" Amy said in a hopeful voice.

They all looked under the bed and behind the table, but there was no unicorn. Jessica could see that Amy looked very disappointed. Jessica felt sorry for her. She would hate to lose her koala bear. She would hate to lose any of her toys.

"Come on, let's think of something else," she said, standing up again.

"I wonder where the others are looking," Ellen said. "We shouldn't look in the same places they already did."

"They won't tell us!" Amy laughed. "It's a race."

"But I can't think of anything else that leans over but doesn't fall," Jessica complained. "The riddle is just too confusing."

Ellen nodded. "Maybe Great-Aunt Helen can give us another clue," she said. "An easier one."

"Good idea," Amy agreed. "Let's ask her."

They ran down the stairs. Jessica was hoping that Great-Aunt Helen would give the clue just to their team. But she knew that wasn't fair.

And besides, the other team was standing right at the bottom of the steps.

"Did you find it?" Lila asked.

Jessica shook her head. "We need another clue."

"So do we," Elizabeth said. "This is a hard riddle. We thought it might be the clock in the den because the pendulum swings back and forth."

"But that's not leaning," Amy pointed out.

"It wasn't there, anyway," Eva said.

"Come on," said Jessica. "Let's ask Great-Aunt Helen for another clue."

Together, they went into the kitchen, where Great-Aunt Helen was reading the newspaper. "Did you solve the riddle?" she asked.

"None of us found the unicorn," Jessica said. "Can you give us an easier clue?"

"Yes, please?" the others said in a chorus.

Great-Aunt Helen took her glasses off. "OK. I want each team to get a piece of paper and a pencil."

Jessica and Elizabeth ran to the telephone

message pad. They each took a piece of paper and grabbed a pencil.

"Ready," Elizabeth said, sitting down.

Jessica sat down, too, and got ready to write. The two teams crowded around the twins to watch and listen. It was a little bit like taking a test at school, but a lot more fun.

"Here you go," Great-Aunt Helen said. "Write down these words. Reading, Enjoying, Cozy, Lounging, Inside, Napping, Easy, Relaxing."

Jessica stared at the words on her paper. "What does it mean?" she asked.

"Do all these words describe the thing that leans over but doesn't fall?" Elizabeth asked.

"Correct," Great-Aunt Helen said. "And the order of the words is important, too."

Everybody stared at the clues. Jessica

couldn't think of what they could possibly mean.

"Hey!" Amy piped up. "Look at the first letter of each word!"

"R-E-C-L-I—" Elizabeth read out loud.

Jessica broke in. "N-E-R!"

"It leans over but it doesn't fall," Eva said.

"RECLINER!" they all shouted at once.

CHAPTER 9

Great-Aunt Helen to the Rescue

All six girls dashed into the living room. Elizabeth was the first to reach the recliner. She got down on her hands and knees to look under it.

"Is it there?" Ellen asked excitedly.

Elizabeth shook her head.

Amy and Lila both looked behind it.

"Here it is!" they yelled at the same time.

Elizabeth jumped up and clapped her hands. "Hurray!" she shouted.

"I can't believe we didn't think of the recliner before." Jessica laughed. "Now the first clue seems easy."

"*Leans over but doesn't fall,*" Eva said. She sat in the recliner and pushed back until the chair opened up.

Elizabeth looked over at the door to the kitchen. Great-Aunt Helen was standing in the doorway, smiling at them.

"Well?" Great-Aunt Helen asked. "Which team won?"

Lila and Amy looked at each other. "We found it at the same time," Lila said.

"So both teams won," Great-Aunt Helen said. "That sounds like the fairest outcome." She walked back into the kitchen and came out again with the first unicorn.

Amy put the unicorn from behind the recliner on the table. Great-Aunt Helen put

the other one next to it. They still looked exactly alike.

"Can you tell which one is which?" Great-Aunt Helen asked Amy and Lila.

Both girls shook their heads. "Then each of you take one."

For a minute, Lila looked like she was about to complain. Then she shrugged and smiled. "I guess it doesn't matter," she said, reaching for the unicorn closer to her.

Amy took the other one and hugged it. "I love you, Princess," she said, giving the unicorn a kiss on its nose.

"Now, how about that dessert?" Great-Aunt Helen reminded everyone. "Is the ice cream parlor all right with everyone?"

"YES!" six voices shouted together.

Elizabeth laughed. She was having so

much fun that she wanted the slumber party to last forever.

"Then let's go," Great-Aunt Helen said, clapping her hands together briskly. "Hurry up. Into the car. On the double."

Elizabeth, Jessica, Lila, Amy, Ellen, and Eva all ran outside and climbed into Great-Aunt Helen's car. Elizabeth and Eva sat in the front seat.

"Is everyone in?" Great-Aunt Helen asked as she turned the key in the ignition. "All six of you?"

"No, eight," Lila spoke up.

Great-Aunt Helen turned around, looking surprised. "Eight? But there were only six of you last time I counted."

Smiling, Lila and Amy held up their unicorns. "You forgot to count these," Amy said.

"Of course," Great-Aunt Helen chuckled.

"Don't let them out of your sight, or we'll have to start the scavenger hunt all over again."

Elizabeth moved closer to Great-Aunt Helen and hugged her arm. "This is the best slumber party ever," she said happily. "Thank you."

"I hope you invite me to the next one," Great-Aunt Helen said.

Elizabeth nodded. "It's a deal."

CHAPTER 10

Sleepyheads

When they got back from the ice cream parlor, the girls went into the den. Jessica flopped down onto her sleeping bag.

"I'm full," she said, holding her stomach.

"Me, too," Eva said, groaning. "I can't believe I ate that whole big sundae."

Amy giggled. "I can. We did a lot of running around today, and worked up a big appetite."

Everyone laughed.

"Let's get ready for bed," Elizabeth said. "We can play guessing games in the dark before we go to sleep."

Jessica hugged her koala bear and smiled. The slumber party was even better than she had thought it would be. Everybody was happy and having a great time. And it was all thanks to Great-Aunt Helen. Jessica decided that Great-Aunt Helen was the best great-aunt in the world.

They arranged the sleeping bags in a circle, with their heads in the center. They got inside with their stuffed animals and made themselves comfortable.

"I want to stay awake all night," Jessica said, trying not to yawn.

"Then you'll have to sleep all day," Lila said.

"I can't sleep all day tomorrow," Amy told everyone. "My mom is taking me shopping for a new Halloween costume."

"I want to be a mermaid this year," Ellen said in a sleepy voice. "With a long tail."

Lila yawned. "Just make sure you'll still be able to walk. I don't know what costume I'll get yet, but my dad says Halloween is going to be special this year."

Jessica closed her eyes. She still wanted to play guessing games, but she was too tired.

One by one, the others stopped talking. Jessica thought someone should turn off the light. But before she knew it, she fell fast asleep.

On Sunday morning, Great-Aunt Helen made waffles for breakfast. Then the twins' friends went home. Elizabeth and Jessica helped Great-Aunt Helen hem Mrs. Wakefield's dresses. Elizabeth held the pincushion, and Jessica was in charge of the scissors.

"When will Mom and Dad and Steven be home?" Jessica asked.

"Pretty soon," Great-Aunt Helen said. "Your parents said they'd be back by four o'clock, and it's nearly two now. And your grandparents are dropping off Steven at six."

"I wish you could stay with us all the time," Elizabeth said, giving her a big smile.

Jessica nodded. "When Mom and Dad go away again, will you come back?"

"I'd love to," Great-Aunt Helen said. She tied a knot in the thread and cut it. The dress that Lila had ripped was all fixed. "Good as new. Even better," she said.

Jessica heard a car door slam. "They're home!" she shouted, jumping up.

Elizabeth and Jessica ran to the door. Mr. and Mrs. Wakefield walked in and hugged each twin tightly.

"Did you have a good slumber party?" Mr. Wakefield asked.

Jessica and Elizabeth looked at each other and then at Great-Aunt Helen. At the same time they both said, "Great!"

When Jessica and Elizabeth walked into their classroom on Monday, a group of boys was making spooky sounds outside the door. Elizabeth could hear them all the way down the hall.

"What are they doing?" Jessica wondered.

"I don't know," Elizabeth said.

The boys were all crowded around someone. Elizabeth squeezed through. Lila was standing in front of Charlie Cashman, glaring at him.

"Quit it, Charlie," Lila said. "Just because you don't believe Hathway Manor is haunted doesn't mean it isn't."

"What are you talking about?" Jessica asked.

"My dad is giving a Halloween party at Hathway Manor," Lila explained. "He said I could invite everyone in class, but I don't think *I* want to go."

"Lila's afraid of the ghost," Charlie said, laughing.

Hathway Manor was an old house that had belonged to the Hathway family for over one hundred years. No one lived there now, and people said a ghost haunted the house.

Part of the house had been turned into a

museum, and the other part was rented out for special occasions, like parties.

"Well, I'm not afraid of ghosts," Jessica said. "I can't *wait* for Halloween!"

Is Hathway Manor really haunted? Find out in Sweet Valley Kids #23, **LILA'S HAUNTED HOUSE PARTY.**

SWEET VALLEY KIDS

Jessica and Elizabeth have had lots of adventures in *Sweet Valley High* and *Sweet Valley Twins*...now read about the twins at age seven! You'll love all the fun that comes with being seven—birthday parties, playing dress-up, class projects, putting on puppet shows and plays, losing a tooth, setting up lemonade stands, caring for animals and much more! It's all part of SWEET VALLEY KIDS. Read them all!

☐	SURPRISE! SURPRISE! #1	15758-2	$2.75/$3.25
☐	RUNAWAY HAMSTER #2	15759-0	$2.75/$3.25
☐	THE TWINS' MYSTERY TEACHER # 3	15760-4	$2.75/$3.25
☐	ELIZABETH'S VALENTINE # 4	15761-2	$2.75/$3.25
☐	JESSICA'S CAT TRICK # 5	15768-X	$2.75/$3.25
☐	LILA'S SECRET # 6	15773-6	$2.75/$3.25
☐	JESSICA'S BIG MISTAKE # 7	15799-X	$2.75/$3.25
☐	JESSICA'S ZOO ADVENTURE # 8	15802-3	$2.75/$3.25
☐	ELIZABETH'S SUPER-SELLING LEMONADE #9	15807-4	$2.75/$3.25
☐	THE TWINS AND THE WILD WEST #10	15811-2	$2.75/$3.25
☐	CRYBABY LOIS #11	15818-X	$2.75/$3.25
☐	SWEET VALLEY TRICK OR TREAT #12	15825-2	$2.75/$3.25
☐	STARRING WINSTON EGBERT #13	15836-8	$2.75/$3.25
☐	JESSICA THE BABY-SITTER #14	15838-4	$2.75/$3.25
☐	FEARLESS ELIZABETH #15	15844-9	$2.75/$3.25
☐	JESSICA THE TV STAR #16	15850-3	$2.75/$3.25
☐	CAROLINE'S MYSTERY DOLLS #17	15870-8	$2.75/$3.25
☐	BOSSY STEVEN #18	15881-3	$2.75/$3.25
☐	JESSICA AND THE JUMBO FISH #19	15936-4	$2.75/$3.25
☐	THE TWINS GO TO THE HOSPITAL #20	15912-7	$2.75/$3.25
☐	THE CASE OF THE SECRET SANTA (SVK Super Snooper #1)	15860-0	$2.95/$3.50

SWEET VALLEY TWINS™

- ☐ BEST FRIENDS #1 .... 15655-1/$2.99
- ☐ TEACHER'S PET #2 .... 15656-X/$2.99
- ☐ THE HAUNTED HOUSE #3 .... 15657-8/$2.99
- ☐ CHOOSING SIDES #4 .... 15658-6/$2.99
- ☐ SNEAKING OUT #5 .... 15659-4/$2.99
- ☐ THE NEW GIRL #6 .... 15660-8/$2.95
- ☐ THREE'S A CROWD #7 .... 15661-6/$2.99
- ☐ FIRST PLACE #8 .... 15662-4/$2.99
- ☐ AGAINST THE RULES #9 .... 15676-4/$2.99
- ☐ ONE OF THE GANG #10 .... 15677-2/$2.75
- ☐ BURIED TREASURE #11 .... 15692-6/$2.95
- ☐ KEEPING SECRETS #12 .... 15702-7/$2.99
- ☐ STRETCHING THE TRUTH #13 .... 15645-3/$2.95
- ☐ TUG OF WAR #14 .... 15663-2/$2.75
- ☐ THE OLDER BOY #15 .... 15664-0/$2.99
- ☐ SECOND BEST #16 .... 15665-9/$2.75
- ☐ BOYS AGAINST GIRLS #17 .... 15666-7/$2.99
- ☐ CENTER OF ATTENTION #18 .... 15668-3/$2.75
- ☐ THE BULLY #19 .... 15667-5/$2.99
- ☐ PLAYING HOOKY #20 .... 15606-3/$2.99
- ☐ LEFT BEHIND #21 .... 15609-8/$2.75
- ☐ OUT OF PLACE #22 .... 15628-4/$2.75
- ☐ CLAIM TO FAME #23 .... 15624-1/$2.75
- ☐ JUMPING TO CONCLUSIONS #24 .... 15635-7/$2.75
- ☐ STANDING OUT #25 .... 15653-5/$2.75
- ☐ TAKING CHARGE #26 .... 15669-1/$2.75

Buy them at your local bookstore or use this handy page for ordering:

Bantam Books, Dept. SVT3, 414 East Golf Road, Des Plaines, IL 60016

Please send me the items I have checked above. I am enclosing $_____
(please add $2.50 to cover postage and handling). Send check or money
order, no cash or C.O.D.s please.

Mr/Ms _____

Address _____

City/State _____ Zip _____

Please allow four to six weeks for delivery.   SVT3-9/91
Prices and availability subject to change without notice.